Bly

Bly

Amelie Fajardo

For grandmas, *Lola* Perla, and *Lola* Ebeng,

Salamat po for your love and kindness.

A.O.F.

Table of Contents

Prologue
Get Over It

I'm Nellie Bly. Twelve years old.

Well, my name was "Bly," but it changed when we got adopted by Danny Consaita.

And right now, we are at my foster father's funeral.

Most people cry, but I don't see the point of it.

Just because your foster parent dies, doesn't mean you have to feel sad.

Plus, our real dad already died, so I'm used to this type of thing.

I admit, however, that I feel a little downhearted, even though we were not really close.

I look to my right and see my sister, Daneisha, age 16.

On my left is Archie (ha-ha), age twenty-two.

They both are really sad.

They'll get over it.

I mean, all people will get over it, that's for sure.

When Mr. Consaita was still alive, I didn't feel that place of serenity, that heartbeat of love.

At least, Archie inherits his house, but not his car; it got damaged from the accident.

But I can still see the light.

Chapter 1
Sammy

Three months after the funeral.

I've made a new friend, Sammy.

The reason for that is because she just moved here and doesn't fret so much about my "loss"; she understands me more.

Most kids at school have been comforting me.

I don't actually need comforting, though, and it's really just annoying.

I was chatting online with Sammy today.

Sam-banana whassup?

killy not much

Sam-banana my siblings r driving me cray

Sam-banana i ll be sent to an erly grave

Sam-banana sorry that was a bit mean i shouldnt have said that

killy ur doin better than how archies doin

Sam-banana im sure his luck will turn around

killy how is the astronaut related?

Sam-banana i dunno?

killy ur so weird

Archie is still in college, studying to become a professional photographer and food stylist, an occupation where you use tools and materials, such as resin and blow dryers, to make food look more appetizing in pictures. I once saw him using glue to stick sprinkles onto donuts.

Every day, he photoshops pictures to perfect his skills. I can tell he works hard and is fully committed to making a career out of it.

He has been trying to get a job as a photographer at well-known magazines and newspapers but-has so far been unsuccessful. Instead, he works a few gigs with shops around town like Cornology, Wired Shop, Jolly Cinema, etc, to build his reputation as a photographer slowly but surely.

"A guy's gotta have a side hustle.", he always said.

I was thinking about this when I realized I was still chatting with Sammy.

Sam-banana helloooooooooooo???

Sam-banana nellie?

killy sorry spaced out

Sam-banana haha lol

killy what?

Sam-banana

killy oh

killy whyyyyyyyyyyyyyyyyyyyyyyyyyyy

Sam-banana hey my sis got a new phone

killy and?

killy aw no not this

Sam-banana

     (This is an inside joke. Sammy and I hate it when people pretend a banana is a phone. Two minutes later we found out there was a Bluetooth device that looked like a banana that connects to your phone. We find it funny now.)

killy haha

killy ur still weird

Sam-banana hey can u help me w/ the hmwrk?

killy ur subconscious:

killy u realizing about when it is due:

Sam-banana u r da worst

Chapter 2
Nine Types of Entertainment

It's Saturday.

As I lay on my bed, I turned my head to the side of my room and looked at everything I own:

These count as eight types of entertainment. For me, at least.

Communicating with spirits using a Ouija board is my ninth type of entertainment.

When I was little, according to the doctors, I apparently had some sort of a mental condition which included symptoms where I had trouble associating with other children, and I saw stuff differently than other people. According to my siblings, I screamed a lot because I had a hard time putting my thoughts into words.

"You probably just have social anxiety. I had that as a kid, too." Danny said as he crumpled up the hospital bills.

Danny believed that the so-called 'mental condition' was just regular kid emotions and the doctors wanted to sell him anti-anxiety pills.

He got me a new doctor who was actually in the medical business to help people, which was the smartest decision he made involving me.

Eventually, my new doctor concluded that I had synesthesia, was just a late talker, and told Danny to send me to a different preschool that had qualified teachers.

Synesthesia is a mental condition where you have blended senses, like seeing numbers as colors.

I didn't think it was synesthesia, but I decided to just use the word to describe whatever problem I had back then.

I saw weird things that only I could see and couldn't put into words. My guess was they were spirits so I started communicating with them using the Ouija board and it actually worked.

At this point, you should know about the rest of my breathing relatives (my siblings).

Daneisha is a science freak and plays tennis.

Archie is a wannabe trendsetter trying to start his own business.

I compare my siblings to the families on TV and think that they switched souls with each other.

Archie is twenty-two, so I guess it's legal for him to "adopt" Daneisha and me.

So now he's like our babysitter but related and not getting paid enough.

Believe it or not, he does look like Archie Andrews, but with glasses and a taste of reality.

And a lot more awkward.

That marks the tenth type of entertainment.

Chapter 3
Our Fridge and the Neighbor's Mentally Challenged Cat

The neighbor's cat is like a piece of sushi in real life.
-He's wild
-He's trouble
But for some reason he has a huge fascination with our fridge.
I don't know why he is not fascinated with his owner's fridge.

(This is not the actual cat. We were never able to catch him. I found this on the internet.)

Maybe we just buy better hot dogs.

Or maybe his owner doesn't feed him well, so he hides in our fridge.

Anyway, it's really annoying.

Annoying like Cookie Monster.

Speaking of food, our eating habits are starting to go downhill.

Daneisha stupidly sold our plates and bowls, and I don't know why.

I can hear her muttering in her room about something, but I don't know what about.

Anyway, I digress.

We eat out of mugs now, which limits our food options, and that totally sucks.

Chapter 4
School Day

Everyone at school always wonders why I'm not constantly crying about my foster dad's death.

That's because I never really knew him.

When he was alive, he took Archie and Daneisha fishing.

But he never took me anywhere.

Whenever he took both of my siblings out, he always hired a babysitter.

When I asked him to sign a field trip form, he kept muttering that he was busy.

I missed out on the ski trip, the amusement park, the bookstore, the chocolate factory, the British Museum (long story), etc.

So, I was sad when he died, but we weren't that close.

I try to explain this to the kids at my school, but they just smile sympathetically at me and go back to watching YouTube.

YouTube was a big thing at my school. It was like the center of life.

In fact, that's all anyone chats about during computer class instead of listening to the teacher.

Actually, we all already know how to use a Chromebook, and the teacher knows this, too.

So basically, computer class is an extra recess, so we all chat online.

dadalaydee yo check it everybody:

killy been there done that

anima_1_over who asked

wut_up hey kelly wanna meet @ the cafe

anima_1_over sure :)

belladona YEAAAH THIS PLACE NEEDS SOME LOOOOOVE

goldfishperson what is ur problem

dadalaydee yo check it

Sam-banana fan club rules!

ava_Cado nerds

Sam-banana :P

superman_&_others I RULE DA WORLD

aaaaaaaaaaaa dude ur annoying

dadalaydee yo join the sixteens fan club after school 2day

Sam-banana yeah:):):):):):):):)

Chapter 5
Snoopy

Sammy is weird.

She convinced me to spy on Kelly Cradshaw and Harlod Jet at the café.

I agreed to come along only because I wanted to eat a New-York-style bagel after she got bored spying..

Also because seventh-grade dates are fun to watch fall apart.

The café kinda looked like the playset in that American Girl Catalog, except human sized.

But there was a blue-haired barista.

I know that blue-haired barista, but that's

another story.

So anyway, Harold started talking to Kelly, and it started to get pretty boring.

All they were talking about was movies.

Sammy wanted to make things interesting, so she pushed me toward them.

I theatrically fell on my face.

Harold looked surprised. "Hey?" he said.

"You won't speak of this."

"Are you that girl from school?"

"What girl?"

"Um…you know. That girl."

"I have a name."

"Uhh…Killy?"

"That is my screen name."

"I think I've seen you before. Are you the girl who hangs out with the barista at the end of the alley?"

"No."

I'm actually lying to Harold here.

A few hours after our wonderful conversation, I met with that barista in the dark alley next to the café.

Her name is Snoopy. She is seventeen years old and sells me boxes of her stuff, which are surprisingly in-new condition every month. She charges me ten dollars and a sugar straw every time I see her.

It's kind of a subscription, but a little shady. I have been on this subscription for three months now.

In fact, this subscription gave me the only things I own right now besides my Ouija board.

After she gave me the box, she sucked from the sugar straw, pretending it was a cigarette.

"Can I ask why you are giving me your old stuff?" I asked.

"Can I ask why you're not sad that your foster dad died?" asked Snoopy.

"Touché. You go first."

"You have a smart mouth. I need to get rid of all these stuff, you're the only kid that will go near this dark alley. Most tweens are weak."

Snoopy looks at me. "Your move."

"I never really knew him. He never paid me any attention. So how can I feel sad?"

"That's a good reason."

"Of course, I'm sad that his life ended, but I don't really feel regrets."

"Okay. Now ya better skedaddle. I hear a dog coming."

I turned to leave, but then she added a side note.

"This monthly thing is now a two-weekly thing." she called out.

"Why?" I asked.

"I need to get rid of this stuff fast."

"How much of this "stuff" do you have?"

"I'm not tellin'. Now go."

Snoopy is one of those people who have that Fuggedaboutit accent, making her sound like a bad guy.

But all she really does is smoke sugar straw cigarettes.

Chapter 6
Daneisha

It has been four weeks since my conversation with Snoopy, and my variety of entertainment is growing.

I was categorizing and organizing my collection in my room when Daneisha came in.

"Hey squirt."

Because she was older, Daneisha never spent a lot of time with me. So, it was a little shocking that she came into my room.

I didn't say anything, but she continued to speak.

"I…got you a present."

She handed me a book.

"Thanks," I said. But she already left.

I don't know why it is so hard for Daneisha to be nice to me.

I read the first three chapters before a line of synesthesia started coming into my mind, and suddenly the words of the book started to look like little animals.

I was entertained for a while, but my eyes started to strain, so I stopped.

I decided to give Daneisha a present, too.

I came into her room. She was in the middle of watching YouTube on her bed.

"Hi."

She looked at me.

"Ever heard of knocking?"

"Oh. Sorry."

I walked through her door, closed it, and knocked.

Even though I couldn't see her, I could hear her slapping her palm on her forehead.

"Come in."

I came in and looked at her YouTube search.

She slapped my hand. "What do you want?"

I didn't feel any pain, so I could give her my gift calmly without screaming hysterically.

I dumped all the cookies on her clean, crisp, bedsheet. Now a mess of crumbs were scattered all over her blankets like stars.

"Here you go, Daneisha. Oops."

To:tad_gravel@gmali.com

From:archie_consaita@gmali.com
Subject: New Home

Dear Uncle Tad,

Our foster dad, Danny Consaita has died four months ago, and right now I'm taking care of Daneisha and Nellie by myself.
Daneisha has gotten over the funeral and is fine with her studies and spends a lot of time on YouTube.
Nellie is surprisingly acting normal like Danny hadn't died at all.
They are independent, but they can still be a handful.
I was wondering if you, Ally and Dave, and Gerald would like to move in with us.
I know that your house is pretty small, and ours has extra space.
I also need to pay off my loan and get a job, so I need extra time and help.
Please consider.

-Archie

Chapter 7
More Chatter

tamer.of.youtube hey its that guy w/ da
weird hair

killy cant argue w/ dat

dadalaydee yo check dees vids

ava_cado STOP SPAMMING THE CHAT

ava_cado   EVERYONE VOTE OUT DADALAYDEE

(dadalaydee got voted out)

Sam-banana im his friend and even I thought this was annoying

giraffe_iso i like chocolate & oreos

colorfulbottlebeer i like socks

qwerty who asked

killy i like season three of #thewalkingdead

black&white ...what?

qwerty hey does anyone wanna join the school newspaper?

colorfulbottlebeer tell me what is happening at dis school that is interesting?

qwerty the school newspaper is not about the school

qwerty its about the things that happen
in this small town

qwerty also includes comics

qwerty including reviews about cat mugs
& socks with colorful beer bottles &
crochet dogs. Figs:

scienceman do we get paid?

qwerty we give one dollar a day to the
people who look on google to find
images for articles

qwerty and one dollar a day to the people who find evidence on cryptids

bocce that is weirdly specific

Sam-banana hey our soccer game is on tue

Sam-banana were playing against the fat cats

m.a.r.s.h.m.a.ll.o.w ur team suks

bocce why is ur names so long?

c☺☺kie hey the fat cats r like 10 yr-olds

c☺☺kie u can win ez

killy one of the players on the opposing team is possessed

killy if the spirit is vengeful on the kids we will win

killy if the spirit is vengeful on us we will lose

killy if the spirit is angry it will kill all of us

ava_cado WAIT WHAT????????

killy if u want i can sacrifice something to get the spirit on our side

killy does anyone have a live bird that they r not emotionally attached to?

killy nm i'll go two the bird shop

Sam-banana thx nellie

Sam-banana that is not morbid @ al

Chapter 8
Sacrifice

I was serious about the sacrifice.

After school, I took Sammy to my house, and we did a séance.

The spirits said that they were on the Fat Cats' side.

Sammy was a little creeped out by this but was impressed how I could communicate with spirits.

"So, the spirits have possessed a girl with gifted soccer skills. If we sacrifice a live animal, the spirits will spread the skill among us equally," I said.

Sammy looked at me skeptically. "Don't you think that there is some natural soccer talent in this girl?"

"Yes, there is some. But a few days ago, a confused spirit that also has natural soccer skills

wandered into her home while she was sleeping and gave her even more soccer skills by possessing her, making her unnaturally skilled at soccer. This double-dipping can cause more unnatural things happening on Earth. Also a few deaths."

"WHAT???? HOW DO YOU KNOW THIS?"

"The spirits told me."

Sammy slapped her forehead.

"So, you're saying that by moving a piece of glass on the alphabet board-"

"Ouija board."

"-you know about all this?"

"Yeah."

Sammy ponders this for a moment.

"Okay. Let us make a sacrifice," she says with a sigh.

We decided to sacrifice a bird.

We went inside a pet shop, and Sammy instantly had a cuteness overload.

"Can't we sacrifice something else?" she asked. "Now I feel guilty. Maybe a chocolate?"

"Actually, we can do that."

"Why didn't you say so?"

"I never actually made a sacrifice before. I'm an amateur."

So, we went to a chocolate store.

Image not supported here because I couldn't take a picture with the crowd of kids around the chocolate shop

We looked at a few things and admired the wrappers.

"We have to find something close to an animal," I said.

"Well, the chocolate is made of milk already," Sammy observed about the nutrition facts.

Then she looked at one of the displays.

She nudged me, I looked at the display, and said, "Maybe some livestock?"

We picked out a chocolate pig with marshmallow filling and went back to my house.

“So how do we sacrifice this thing?” asked Sammy.

“I guess we just put it in front of the Ouija board and wait.”

I put the pig in front of the board.

After a few minutes, nothing happened.

So, I showed Sammy my wonderful selection of entertainment.

After half an hour, the pig was still in front of my Ouija board.

“What is taking so long?” Sammy looked a little bored.

I moved the glass piece a little bit, then watched it as it started to move without my help.

"Thanks."

The pig caught flame and incinerated.

When it disappeared, I looked at the board as the piece started to move again.

"Everyone will get out alive. Soccer games."

I turned to look at Sammy, but she was petrified and pale.

Chapter 9
Archie

The next day was Saturday.

I walked downstairs to get my daily dose of mug food.

The fridge and pantry were practically empty except for a few things.

"My-Cup-Of-Cake." I read aloud the packaging.

Daneisha came down the stairs. "You don't have to read so loud. You can already read quietly, can't you? Aren't you already twelve? Where is all the food?"

"I dunno."

I was eating the cake when I heard the doorbell.

Daneisha went to the door. I could hear her opening it and some indistinct chatter.

When she came back, I asked, "Who was there?"

"Nobody."

I decided to shut up. When Daneisha is vague about something, it's better to not ask her questions.

Archie, seeming to appear out of the blue, ran to the door and brought in an Indonesian girl his age in a wheelchair.

I followed him into his studio, where he had a little table set up with his camera equipment.

Archie was chatting with the girl in the wheelchair.

The girl looked behind him and pointed at me knowingly. Archie turned around.

"Hey Nellie. This is Jordan, my co-worker." he said.

Jordan waved.

I looked at her, then said something stupid.

"You look like Jordan from that graphic novel… Never mind, I forgot which one.

Archie gave me a dirty look, so I changed the subject.

"Whatcha' doin'?" I asked.

"We're making some pictures."
"Well, you're copying one of the pages in my book."

"How so?"

"Well, you put soap in the orange juice to make it look freshly poured then intentionally shaped the bacon with foil then put a circle of cardboard in the bowl and put white glue on the circle then sprinkled the cornflakes on the glue and then trimmed the pancakes 'cause they were irregularly shaped then sprayed them with furniture spray then pinned the blueberries on the stack of pancakes then heated up the syrup so it becomes thicker then molded clay on the bread to make it look like avocados and molded other pieces of clay to look like differently cooked eggs then painted and sprayed them."

Archie put up a finger up to protest but realized *Oh man this kid is onto me* and gave me a grocery list.

"Can you please go to the grocery store?" he said, rubbing his forehead, obviously overwhelmed, the food stylist that he is.

"Actually, I was going to meet up with Sammy for homework," I replied.

"Can you multitask?"

"Yes."

"Money's on the counter."

I took the money; I was going to meet Snoopy on my way, so I took a little extra.

Before I closed the front door, I yelled a side note.

"OH YEAH YOU CAN PHOTOGRAPH MY THINGS JUST PLEASE DON'T BREAK ANYTHING."

I closed the door. Although I couldn't see them, I could hear Archie and Jordan laughing hysterically while shouting, "SHE READ MY MIND!"

The pictures Archie took of my things were actually pretty good.

Chapter 10
Books

I invited Sammy to the grocery store so we could do homework while grocery shopping. For English, we had to review the books we recently read.

Sammy pushed the cart.

"What did Hephastios do to catch Aphrodite and Ares cheating?" I asked.

"Can we move onto something less awkward?"

"Megalodon teeth are as big as? Pasta."

Sammy put pasta in the cart.

"An adult human's hand."

"What did Hera do to Hephastios when he was born? Chicken tenders."

Photo by Layerlab

Sammy put chicken tenders in the cart.

"She threw him off Olympus."

"What evidence did they find of Amelia Earhart's disappearance? Gummy bears."

"Her skeleton and shoes."

"Gummy bears in England are called? My Cup Of Cake mix."

"Dancing bears."

"Harry Potter's godfather is? Cereal."

"Sirius Black. Okay, my turn. The national bird of Guatemala is?"

"The Quetzal. Avocados."

It went back and forth like this for a while, bear facts and Harry Potter trivia.

By the time we were done studying, our cart was full.

Chapter 11
Qwerty

So, it's Monday.
Back at school I decided to join some extracurricular activities.

I decided to join the school newspaper, since I was good at finding images on the internet.
After school I came to Tharisa, screen name "qwerty".
"Hey Nellie."
"'Sup."
"So, what position do you want?"
"Images person."
"'Kay. See you tomorrow."

Sammy was listening in on our conversation.

"HOW DID YOU DO THAT?"

"Stop yelling. And what are you talking about?"

"Tharisa never gives someone a spot in the newspaper without punching them in the face. She has high standards."

"You're making this up."

"Would I lie?"

"You do. A lot."

<u>The Weekly Post</u>

COMPOST FOUND IN CAFETERIA COOKIES

The lunch ladies are betraying us. One of the 8th grade students reported seeing compost remains in his chocolate chip cookie he bought from the cafeteria options. We got three new reports from
other students. We're all about recycling, but let's get real.

Photo by Gio Bartlett

Chapter 12
Cryptids

I finished up my newspaper images duties and walked to the field where Sammy would have her soccer game.

On my way there, I passed this sign:

Geez, how stupid can people get?

So anyway, the fourth graders were crushing the game, so Sammy was rocking back and forth on the bench, hands in her face, muttering how humiliating it was to get beaten by younger kids.

We were walking home in silence.

"At least nobody died." I commented.

Sammy looked at me and gave me a hug.

I showed her some photos on my phone that Archie made.

"These would make good profile photos," observed Sammy.

"I'll email you some more photos later."

"Wait. What was that sound?"

"Probably the Basilisk, Harry Potter."

"No, seriously! I heard something."

"It's the female taxidermist, Paddington Bear."

"Will you stop joking around?"

"Will the humans eat Frank?"

"I swear. I feel something is following us."

"It's the evil banker, little Bank child."

"Please don't mention that R-rated movie that we watched. And I do hear something."

I looked around, but it was hard to see because it was 6 pm and it was dark outside. But I did see a tall silhouette in front of Sammy.

I guessed that it was a tree.

"There is a tree behind you," I said.

I turned on the flashlight on my phone and pointed up at the tree.

Expecting to see a tree, I saw instead a gorilla-like creature seven feet tall with brown hair.

Sammy looked behind her back and saw this creature and knocked me over, running and screaming like a constipated wiener dog.

Then I saw that I was on the same street as the Bigfoot sign.

I was still on the ground when I looked up at what was supposedly Bigfoot.

Bigfoot, alarmed by the light from my phone, ran away like a silent decapitated chicken.

I made a mental note to look up cryptids.

###

A few days after my encounter with Bigfoot I have been studying cryptids.

And now I'm glad that my encounter was not with something worse.

To:jordan_arya@gmali.com
From: :archie_consaita@gmali.com
Subject: Assignments (aka homework)

Hi Jordan,

Here are some of the pictures that we took last weekend:

This weekend we have to work on our photoshop skills. Is Saturday a good time?
-Archie

To:archie_consaita@gmali.com
From:jordan_arya@gmali.com
Subject: Re: Assignments (aka homework)

Archie-

Sure, Saturday is a good time. At your place or my place?

-Jordan

To:jordan_arya@gmali.com
From:archie_consaita@gmali.com
Subject: Re: Re: Assignments (aka homework)

Jordan-

My place.

-Archie

To:archie_consaita@gmali.com
From:jordan_arya@gmali.com
Subject: Re: Re: Re: Assignments (aka homework)

Archie-

Your place is fine. Your sisters are so funny.

-Jordan

To:killy@gmali.com
From:sam-banana@gmali.com
Subject: hangin'

yo nellie can i hang at your place this sat? great!
my cousin's coming over this sat and hes older and
a huge jerk so can we have a sleepover? thanks
youre a lifesaver

(if its a yes send this image back)

PS what r u goin 2 review 4 the school newspaper

To:sam-banana@gmali.com
From:killy@gmali.com
Subject: sure

why does it have to be a koi fish? NM ur still weird

To:killy@gmali.com
From:sam-banana@gmali.com
Subject: yayyyyyyyyyy

synthesia must me so fudge
sorry i meant "fun" stupid autocorrect
my cousin is so mean once he turned off the lights
after telling me a scary story then he snuck up on
me then i punched him in the gut and everyone
blamed me
:(:(:(
hey u should read a book

To:sam-banana@gmali.com
From:killy@gmali.com
Subject:

hey i named my parrot james perry

Chapter 13
Natural Disasters

Archie had Jordan over again. They were doing something on their computers.

Sammy came over really early. I guess she really hated her cousin.

I was working on my school newspaper reviews when Sammy asked, "Do you wanna re-enact Studio Comedy sketches with your stuffed animals?"

"I only have three stuffed animals, and what's Studio Comedy?"

"I thought you knew about them. You named your parrot James Perry."

"That…is extremely coincidental."

"The original cast of Studio C, Adam Barg, Matt Mease, Mallory Everston, Whitney Cill, Jason Grey, Jeremy Warner, Stephen Mell, James Perry, Stacey Harvey, and Natalie Madisen, left Studio Comedy in season nine, and are now acting sketches in Funny! Studios."

"You sound like you've been preparing this speech for a long time."

"I have."

Then, theatrically, she showed me the T-shirt she was wearing.

I observed it.

"What are Freelancers?"

"JK! Studios."
"I'll look on YouTube later."
"Oh! You can't forget Mark Rubert."
"Fine."
"I hear it's gonna snow overnight."
"Yeah right. It's the middle of March."
"I've got a donut sleigh."

"I've got an all-season sled. We have donuts in the fridge, but you have to use a napkin instead of a plate.

We walked downstairs.

"Dibs on half-half!" yelled Sammy. "A delicious donut consisting of both chocolate and vanilla cake on each half of this doughy pastry.", said Sammy as she titled her chin upwards expressing her inner food critic.

Daniesha was working on her homework on the bar.

"Can you keep your little friend on mute?" she said.

"Hey, are you supposed to be doing homework?" asked Sammy.

"Of course I am. Don't you have homework?"

"No. There's no homework on the weekend."

"Well, this is the real world. It's not like Kiwi Crate or Little Passports."

"I know that you mean that as an insult that we're still little kids, but we actually still do those things," I said honestly. "We keep all the boxes."

"Arrggggh. You are so naive."

"So…how's Archie?" Sammy asked me, munching on a donut.

       "He's studying advertisements and computer stuff and photo taking and photoshopping."

       "He's also a hopeless romantic," added Daneisha.

       Archie, seemingly out of nowhere, bolted into the room and interjected emphatically, "There is nothing between me and Jordan!"

       "Jordan *and I*," Daneisha corrected.

       "STOP LOOKING AT MY COMPUTER."

       "Nice getup, penguin.

       "I didn't change a thing about my daily T-shirt and jeans fashion."

       "You've been practicing your hot cocoa skills, taking pictures for extra credit.

       "You...you can't prove anything!"

       "Can we get a snake?" I asked. Sammy was looking weirdly at Archie and Daniesha like teenagers were the apocalypse.

       Archie looked at me funny. "You can't even take care of an ant farm and you expect me to trust you with a snake?"

"Only ten percent of all snake species are venomous." I added.

Archie left the room.

Sammy and I watched a bit of Queer Eye.

Archie interrupted us and lectured that "we were only twelve and you should just watch something else that show is rated TV-14."

To which I reply honestly, "You swear more than the Fab 5. Okay fine, we'll watch something else."

Being the honest person I am, we watched *Some Assembly Required* and *Austin and Ally*.

An hour after we fell asleep, Sammy woke up to go to the bathroom, and when she came back, she shook me awake.

"Nellie, there's a ghost in your room!" she yelled.

Still groggy, I said, "That's just your dream on top of reality."

“NO, I SAW IT, I SWEAR.”

“Stop yelling. You’re gonna wake up Daneisha and Archie.”

Then the ground started shaking.

The shaking started to increase.

I comically fell out of bed.

“What the heck?”

The shaking got pretty intense.

Sammy was holding onto the walls, as that would’ve helped.

After a minute, this earthquake made it feel like the world around me was churning like butter.

Strangely, I felt warm, with no alarm of this natural disaster.

Damn synesthesia.

It suddenly stopped with no warning.

Sammy let go of the walls, gasping for air.

She pulled out an inhaler.

“Asthma attack,” she said, and took two puffs.

Archie ran into my room.

“Nellie are you okay?” he asked.

“Yeah…this whole experience felt like a mug of hot cocoa…”

“It’s just synesthesia. How about you, Sammy?”

“Yeah, I’m good. Just had a minor asthma attack.”

“Do you want me to drive you home?”

“Nah. I’ll be okay.”

Surprisingly, nothing fell from the shelves or even moved from its place during the earthquake.

Everything was still intact.

I checked to see that my things were still in their place in on the shelf at the end of my room.

"skajdsvsdvsgfwyefdsghhsdghjadgdavhdjgsghdjghgdahjahdaghdaghdgahhjdaghghjdajdgajnfvekfjjjjjjjjjjjj jjjjlskdkdsklqeeiieiiowirhrhehfheuuhfufuhfehufuhfhieuhfeifuhuiehifueheuifhieuhfiehfeuihfehiupaipidiadijdjjsidjsijdiwjeiuu rureiruiueurureib ijfiewjoowrivirhrwhu" I murmured, secretly thanking my school for providing the Kiwi Crate and Little Passports, my mother for the Ouija board, Archie for the ant farm even though it has dead ants, Daniesha for twelve again and the hand-me-down Chromebook, Sammy for the books, and Snoopy for everything else.

I ran down the hall and barged into Archie's room.

The photo guy he is, his printer, bean bag chair, and his Chromebook didn't move an inch, all in the same place.

Even the loose pieces of paper where he printed color pictures of photoshopped animal hybrids, and my colorful possessions were still on his desk.

Catching a glimpse of a picture of my mother, I held it in my hands.

I stared at it. She looked a lot like me.

The picture was probably taken a long time ago, since she died before I turned two.

I heard my name being called, so I dropped the photo in its place and ran downstairs.

Chapter 14
Aftershock

Everyone went back to sleep thirty minutes after the earthquake.

I woke up, Sammy was still in our house. She was going to stay at my place for the rest of the day.

Archie was photographing kiddie meals on the table at breakfast.

"Use the bar," he said.

On the bar was Archie's computer. On his computer were hybrid animals.

Sammy liked those photos.

"Whatcha doin', Archie?" asked Sammy.

"I'm taking a few advertisement pictures. Once I have a full set of photos, my career will finally take off," he said dreamingly.

"Or finally exist." Daneisha walked in.

Archie ignored her and kept on taking pictures.

###

"You gotta send me Archie's photo page," Sammy said enthusiastically.

"I don't think it's done yet," I replied.

"No wonder he takes pictures of your things." Sammy strapped on her helmet. "You have such great taste in color." She stripped on elbow and knee pads.

"Thanks. Archie has good color taste, too." I pumped my bike. "I can't wait to see his finished file." I put on my helmet.

Sammy wanted to go to the park because it was a beautiful sunny day.

Sammy strapped on her roller blades and waited for me outside. I rode out on a Schwinn bike.

"So, I think that we should first ride a few rounds around the cement loop, then we can catch frogs by the creek." Sammy drew an imaginary route in the air.

"Can we interview those sixteen-year-olds that hang out there? Tharisa asked me to get a scoop on what teens want in their schools."

"Ugh, fine. But can we be subtle?"

"Okay."

We rode to the park on the route Sammy had planned.

When we arrived at the creek, Sammy caught a few frogs in her bucket.

I accidentally caught a water snake in my bucket.

I told Sammy that we should take a break and interview the sixteen-year-olds, who were hanging out by the creek, too. But they were having a little party, even though there were only four of them.

We didn't know any of their names, but we knew that "girl in the ponytail" was dating "dude who you see working in all the shops and restaurants" and "sunglasses guy" was dating "peaceful she-man."

Sammy was not on board with talking to the teenagers, but I told her we could hide under the picnic table they were using and overhear their conversation instead.

Sammy hated teenagers, but she does like pretending to be a superspy.

So, we swiftly moved and hid under their table.

I took out my tape recorder so I could tape every word the teenagers said.

The teenagers sat down on the ledge of the table.

Their conversation was something like this, according to the recording. I also found out what their real names were:

Fiona: So, are you all going to comic con with me?
Stevie: Wouldn't miss it!
Mark: Not Really..I only have a Yoda costume.
(Stevie bursts out laughing)
Mark: It's not mine! It's Jessi's!
(Stevie falls over and rolls on the ground)
Mark (changing the subject): So, what do you miss about school?
Bailey: What's so good about school today?
Mark: I meant middle school.
Stevie (pulled himself together): I miss the Happy Meals and the Kid Cuisine stuff. And the shortbread cookies. And hotdog Fridays. And they were chicken hotdogs! With cheese!
Fiona: All you think about is food.
Mark: The computer classes were fun. Chatting online really is more like a diary.
Fiona: Nobody really posts puberty in the chat, dude.
(Mark throws a chicken nugget at her.)
Stevie: I remember that there was a sugar glider as a class pet..he was named Napoleon! And that parrot in the science room…
Bailey: Call me crazy, but I kinda' miss those Little Passports and Kiwi Crates things.
Me (in a whisper): Great. I got everything I need. Let's—
Mark: Hey guys, my sister dominated a soccer game.
Stevie: Your sister always dominates soccer games.

Mark: Yeah, but she dominated this game. And she was competing with kids three grades higher than her!
Fiona: Okay, that doesn't happen often.

Sammy looked like a brick had hit her in the face.

"Hey. This is probably a different game." She gave herself a pep talk.

Fiona: What was your sister's team's name again?
Mark: The Fat Cats. They were competing against our middle school team. I guess that our middle school now has some very bad players.
Bailey: Troof.
Stevie: Compared to how the team played when we were in middle school, I guess that must be humiliating. How did the elementary kids get paired up to play against our middle school kids?
Fiona: According to my sister, she was spectating the game, the middle school team was lagging behind compared to other middle school teams, so they needed something to warm them up.

I turned off the recording app.
Sammy already jumped up from under the table.

"IF NELLIE BLY DIDN'T SACRIFICE A CHOCOLATE PIG TO THE SPIRIT THAT POSSESSED YOUR SISTER, SHE WOULD'VE EXPERIENCED SOMETHING MORE THAN LOSING OUR GAME. I WAS PLAYING AGAINST HER KNOWING THAT WE SAVED HER LIFE."

Mark looked at her perplexedly. "What is your deal, kid?"

Bailey was no help calming Sammy's nerves. "It's spirits wanting to confuse us."

Fiona apparently listened to Sammy's wonderful speech. "Nellie Bly? Like, that girl mentioned in the Judy Moody book?"

"That is entirely coincidental." Sammy held up one finger.

Stevie blew his chance to get out of the area. "Um, ma'am, I'm trying to be polite here, this is teenager stuff we're doing here. And you don't look like a teenager..." he said, acting nervous.

I popped my head up from the table, holding my recording.

"Seems to me you miss middle school." I waved the tape over my head.

In that time, I was talking to the teenagers, Sammy walked back to the creek, picked up my bucket, and walked back to the table.

Luckily, I was able to shelter myself under the table before Sammy threw the bucket at Bailey, Mark, Fiona, and Stevie.

I forgot to pour it out into the creek before we hid under the picnic table, so there was still water in it.

So was the snake.

<u>The Weekly Post</u>

TEENAGERS ATTACKED BY SNAKES

Photo by The New York Public Library

Last Sunday, four teenagers, Stevie Boham, Fiona Renton, Mark Rotner, and Baily Baxter were attacked by a snake that was thrown in a bucket at them by someone anonymous. Luckily, none of them were hurt, just slight life scarring.

BIGFOOT SPOTTED AFTER SOCCER GAME

Nellie Bly and Sammy Greenwood were walking down Pembrooke Ave when a hairy figure seven feet tall stood by

them, for some reason not being noticeable.

EXCLUSIVE: TEENAGERS DISH THAT THEY MISS MIDDLE SCHOOL

They miss our Little Passports and Kiwi Crates!

The food here used to be good & Happy glass used to be allowed!

There was a parrot and a sugar glider as class pets! Why do we get the goldfish?

Chapter 15
Oreo

I woke up on Monday, pretty groggy.

I start my day looking around my room, dark cornflower blue colored walls, looking at my things on matching shelves.

Colorful. Color-coordinated.

Yesterday was sunny, so I was hoping that today would be the same.

Shockingly, at first glance at the window from my bed I saw white.

I got out of bed and stood in front of the window.

It seems that it had snowed overnight.

I walked downstairs for breakfast.

After I packed my lunch, I opened the door.

Apparently, it had snowed a whopping twelve inches.

I cleaned the floor after I closed the door.

Archie came down, fully dressed. "It's a snow day today."

"I figured already."

"Wow. A snowstorm in the middle of March." Archie scratched his head. "I think a few animals decided to stay inside the basement. I could hear a few squeaking noises coming from the walls. Make sure they don't get in the kitchen. Can you patch up the hole in the pantry?"

"Sure."

Unlike most houses, our pantry is in the kitchen, not the basement.

Animals could easily get to kitchen from the basement through the hole in the kitchen pantry.

I know this because there is a fourth grader named Jane Wazzer a few blocks down from us, and last summer she asked Daneisha to pet-sit her parrots because they had to have their walls repainted.

Daneisha was one of the many people Jane asked to pet-sit because her mom is a zoologist and keeps a lot of animals at home.

Jane said it was okay to keep them in the basement because it was at the right humidity.

It turns out, there was a hole in the basement that led to our pantry big enough to fit a ten-year-old kid. The parrots discovered it and ended up in our kitchen pantry.

I patched up the hole with a piece of wood and nailed it into the wall.

I then saw the cereal box of Oreo-O's fall to the side by itself.

The top was already open, and a black and white guinea pig scampered out.

I quickly picked it up before it ran into our other food.

I walked to Archie and told him that I found a guinea pig in our cereal box.

He guessed that the little guy discovered the hole before I could patch it.

Before I could ask, he said, "Fine you can keep him.

He turned on his computer.

"There's a spare basket in the pantry."

I was feeding the guinea pig some carrots. I named him Oreo because he appeared out of nowhere.

The carrots were devoured immediately.

Daneisha walked in with a tray of shortbread cookies. Chocolate chip.

I left Oreo in the basket and joined her at the bar.

I read a chapter of *Tales of the Cryptids* when I heard a crunching sound.

I saw Oreo on the table eating one of the cookies.

I was distracted from the fact that Oreo had escaped a two-foot-high basket with a weighted bottom.

I couldn't take him to the vet because of the snow, so Archie assumed the worst.

But the whole day, he didn't throw up.

He was just as happy a little guy as ever before.

He was also a happy little escape artist.

I woke up on Tuesday to see the snow gone and Oreo in the pantry, happily eating the real Oreo O's.

So, I guess that I have a guinea pig that can eat human food.

Chapter 16
Jonah's Grocery

On Tuesday, I had a geography quiz and a science test.

But thanks to the Little Passports and Kiwi Crates, I think I aced them.

But there was also a math test and fitness test.

I say that math is my strong suit, but Gorey Thompson was trying to copy my test.

Now let me say that we had history.

Emphasis on the word "noogie". We were never friends.

So, I quickly scribbled down wrong answers, he copied them and proudly strutted up to the desk, being the first one to finish.

Once he sat back down, I erased all my answers and put in the correct ones.

After school, I walked home with Sammy. She wanted to meet Oreo.

Archie was sitting at the bar reading a *Vogue* magazine.

Archie realized we were there and quickly hid the magazine under the table like he was embarrassed about something.

Sammy ignored Archie's "Hello" and went upstairs with me to my bedroom.

We were staring at the kid next door who sells groceries in a lemonade stand.

This kid is named Jonah.

I have to interview him later for the school newspaper.

Luckily, he is our age, and our interview will be better than we did for the teenagers.

Also, Archie is one of his best customers because his groceries are in good condition.

Archie doesn't trust Starbucks or Goodway anymore after he did a little research on the internet.

I read this page. It involved a dead mouse in a cup of coffee.

After Sammy and I reread the page together, Sammy said that she needed to go home and puke.

She did leave, so I walked to Jonah's little stand to interview him.

Jonah is homeschooled, so I only see him after school.

"Hi Nellie." He waved me over. "I have a good deal on this delectable pastry from Starbread! 15% off!"

"Thanks, Jonah. But I'm broke. And I came here to interview you."

"Shoot your questions. Business is slow today. I've got time."

After my interview with Jonah, customers started to arrive.

I said goodbye to Jonah and walked back to my house to see Archie on the couch, blanket spread over him drinking a soda like it was a beer.

I turned to Daneisha. "It's teenager stuff," she whispered.

Chapter 17
Tharisa

Thursday. Lunch period.

I was telling Sammy about how Archie was acting, and I could tell that she was getting uncomfortable, and not because Tharisa was sitting with us.

According to other people, Tharisa's fists were always in someone's face when you sign up for the school newspaper so she can see if you have the quality for the job.

So basically, that's her way of a survey.

Tharisa lives two doors down from Sammy, who lives across from me.

Sammy is like the spider, and Tharisa is like the broom. Know what I'm saying?

Anyway, I digress.

Tharisa was getting uncomfortable, too. "Hey, put in the school newspaper why don't ya'? Wait — can we do that?"

"I'll discuss it with my sister," I said.

###

Daneisha was comically banging her head on the table when I came home.

"Archie is not opening up to Jordan. No way, no how. ARCHIE, YOU IMBECILE! YOU'RE 22!" she ranted.

"Maybe he just needs a little push," I said.

"How?"

The Weekly Post

ARCHIE CONSAITA IS A HOPELESS WRECK

Unlike Archie Andrews, Archie Consaita, 22, 170 pounds, has no life. Yessir! What he needs is a girlfriend! And specifically, Jordan Arya! Tuesday afternoon he was found on the couch drinking mustard soda! For advice for Archie please leave suggestions in the box at the end of the cafeteria! Please don't leave your name.

@#$%^&*!; MAN FINDS DEAD MOUSE IN HIS COFFEE!

All we can say is that it is gross. Someone is out for you! This doesn't happen on accident!

JONAH'S GROCERIES: FIVE STARS! EXCLUSIVE INTERVIEW

Q: Where do you get all your groceries?

A: I always seem to have extra food in my pantry or fridge. It is shameful to waste it.

Photo collage by Amelie Fajardo

Q: Why do you sell the produce from a lemonade stand?

A: Well, it's the only thing available to put outside that has space for a few coolers and a few baskets.

Q: Why are you homeschooled?
A: I honestly have no idea how that is related to my stand.

Q: Do you sell lemonade?
A: Actually, I do. I offer free samples!

Chapter 18
Oh Damn

I handed Daneisha a copy of the school newspaper after I got home from school on Thursday.

"This is genius!" she shouted after she read the article. "I propose some cookies to celebrate!"

"Sure. Let me get Oreo. I need to take him for a walk. We can eat the cookies outside," I said.

We were outside for a while, just talking in our front lawn, when we heard Archie scream from inside the house.

I looked at Daneisha. "Did you stupidly leave the paper on the kitchen table?"

Daneisha gave me a guilty smile. I slapped my forehead.

We walked inside while Archie waved the paper above our heads.

"I'M NOT DESPERATE!" he yelled. "I'M ALSO NOT HAPPY THAT YOU PUT MY WEIGHT IN THE PAPER!"

"My grade brought you some suggestions.", I said, holding up a few pieces of paper. "And you do sound desperate."

Archie took the suggestions and started to read them, making weird faces at each one.

"Tell her how many things you can shove down your pants and name each item. I suggest using food

brands like the ones from Jonah's Grocery," Archie read aloud. *"Archie you a stupid little donkey. Take her to Harry Potter World.* None of this is useful!"

"I got Jonah to write you one." I handed him another piece of paper."

Archie took it.

"Dear Archie,
Be yourself! A girl should like you the way that you are!

PS: I would put more in this note, but I get uncomfortable when I write stuff like this, and I reached my limit there. Good luck! And maybe get set up with a love consultant!
-Jonah.

PPS: Maybe you're pushing yourself too hard to succeed in life. You're young, so enjoy it while you can! Don't forget to play some video games or swim once in a while and be passionate about your photography!"

Archie paused. "This is the only one that is useful. Yet most ridiculous."

"Can't you just call her?" asked Daneisha.

"I want to be nominated," said Archie.

"I could actually set you up," I said.

Archie looked at me. "You? Says the kid who only chats online and sends grammatically incorrect emails."

"I have a friend at school named Tharisa Arya. Jordan is coincidentally her big sister."

Archie jumped up on the table in a frenzy. "Callooo! Hallelujah!"

"She'll beat you up if you make Jordan cry though."

Archie climbed down from the table. "Calloo. Yay."

To:<u>qwerty@gmali.com</u>
From:<u>killy@gmali.com</u>

hey Tharisa, its Nellie.
and just in case ur suspicious i work for the school newspaper and you hate Cheetos.
so yeah archie doesn't wanna call jordan cause he wants to be nominated.
and who better to say, "oh hey jordan you should totally date archie consaita hes a great guy and is good at photography but his hair looks weird." than you.
and pls no physical beat downs, to ur sister, archie or me. or sammy.

To<u>killy@gmai.com</u>
From:<u>qwerty@gmali.com</u>

hey nells! i'll write an article bout this in the paper nxt week.
and sure i'll set up jordan with archie. she likes coffee. 'wink wink'

To:qwerty@gmali.com
From:killy@gmali.com

archie doesn't drink coffee now that he knows bout
the mouse fiasco
Do u wanna sleep over @ my place?

To:killy@gmali.com
From:qwerty@gmali.com

watching a movie @ home is fine. and sure

Chapter 19
Teenager Stuff

Saturday.

Archie sent me to the Redbox to rent some movies. Sammy came with me because she wanted to avoid her cousin, as he was visiting again.

Since Archie has a date today, and Sammy's cousin was visiting, she was facing a dilemma.

But I guess she hates her cousin more than teenagers, so she decided to have another sleepover at my place, but she was going to stay in my room the whole time the date commenced.

"How many movies do teenagers watch in one sitting?" Sammy whined. I was still renting movies from the Redbox

"Archie gave me a list." I said.

Sammy rushed to the shortbread cookies when I opened my front door.

I handed Archie the movies.

"Stay up in your room the whole time." he instructed. "I am watching movies for mature people only. No offense."

"AKA, he wants to have a romantic setting," added Daneisha.

Sammy gagged upon hearing this but he quickly recovered and said. "Why dontcha just mold the couch in the right position so you can make out?"

"Just stay in your room."

"I invited Tharisa to sleep over, too," I said.

"What? Why didya do that?" asked Sammy, still chewing on her cookies.

"Relax. I told her not to beat you up. And she is really nice when you get to know her."

Sammy loosened her shoulders and grabbed the tray of shortbread cookies. "I'm taking these."

Tharisa arrived thirty minutes later and was immediately dragged up to my room.

Sammy was bored immediately with our entertainment options: Tharisa talking.

It was like she was waiting for innocent souls to listen to her mind.

And she talked about everything like a possessed person. But I knew that this was a natural talent, not a paranormal activity.

But what was paranormal was that her words sounded like pictures.

But that just sounds like my synesthesia kicking in.

Tharisa droned on and on.

Sammy emailed Jonah while I was listening to Tharisa, and he came over ten minutes later.

Tharisa stopped talking when Jonah entered the room.

"I texted him if he wanted to join our sleepover," Sammy explained.

"My mom said yes, but we can't have any junk food.", Jonah said. "And I can't sleep over. I have to come back home."

"So what's the point of coming over?" Tharisa asked,

"Because I get to stay up late like a big kid!"

"You are a big kid."

"No I'm not; I'm only twelve!"

"I say we do some espionage on Archie," Sammy proposed.

"That sounds weird," said Jonah. "And they might be doing that thing with their mouths."

"On their first date?" Tharisa pointed out. "I vote we spy on them."

"Fine."

Everyone looked at me. "Sure. Okay."

All the lights were turned off in the house because Archie wanted to have that cinema vibe, so the only light we had was from the TV screen and from a little electronic candle.

Let's just say that we looked pathetic for a group of "super spies."

We tiptoed down the stairs, but we could've just walked normally because the TV was on full blast.

Archie and Jordan were sitting on the couch, eyes glued to the screen, so it was pretty easy to crawl under the couch, but that was stupid because all four of us couldn't get a good view.

So, we walked back up the stairs and "spied" on Archie and Jordan from the top of the staircase.

It wasn't a very impressive place to sit, since we all wanted to get a good view.

Thirty minutes passed with nothing exciting happening besides in the movie.

Then Archie did the I'm-pretending-to -yawn-so-I-have-an-excuse-to-put-my-arms-up- in-the-air-and-around-your- shoulder move.

If that wasn't revolting enough, they both looked at each other and did "those things with their mouths."

Sammy said a bad word in English, Tharisa swore in Indonesian, and Jonah definitely swore in a language that I didn't know about, and I just said, "I regret helping that guy get this far."

Chapter 20
Help

qwerty nellie, ur brother my sis
permanently scarred me four lyfe

qwerty im not blamin u. im blamin them

killy i regret helping archie

qwerty i regret helping jordan

chocoman hey guys

killy hi jonah

Sam-banana IM NEVER GOIN TO UR HOUSE
AGAIN

Sam-banana
!@#$%^&*&^%$#@!@#$%^&*&^%$#@#$%^&&^%

@#$%^&*&^%$#@!@#$%^&^%$#@

$#@#$%^&*&^%$#@!@#%&%&^(

$#@#$%^&*% $#@#$%^&*@*(*

$#@#$%^&*&^%$#@!$% $#@#$%

$#@#$%^&*&^%$#@!@#$%^&^%$#@#$#!$^%&%&^$*^#%

Sam-banana I WOULDVE RAYHER HEARD
THARISA BLAB ABOUT THEES THINGS MORE
THAN fifty TIMES THAN RE-LIVE THAT

qwerty hey turn off caps lock it feels
like ur screamin in my ear

qwerty and stop rage-chattin with pics.
i can tell u prepared this

Sam-banana ok im calm now

Everyone was imprinting on last night.
That made me think of when I walked to
Snoopy's alley earlier that day to get one of her
boxes.
She was wearing one of those dark
sunglasses.
She lowered them. "What's wrong, sparky?"
"My brother was being gross yesterday."
"I'll look no further for details. How old is he?"
"Twenty-two."
"Well, where I come from, the eldest can do
whatever he wants. Hang in there, kid. It's gonna be a
rough ride."
"How do you know?"
"Trust me. I have a degree in people skills."
I made a confused look on my face.
"Never mind, Nellie. Open the box."
I opened the box.

" Now please tell me what you have gotten from me so far." she said.

"

"

I said.

"What do you have from Archie?"
"An ant farm."
"Daneisha?"
"Hand-me-downs."
"Your mom?"
"A Ouija board."
"Your dad?"
"The couch."
"Now who are your friends?"
"Jonah, Tharisa, and Sammy."
"What do you have from Jonah?"
"Brand food."
"From Tharisa?"
"Slippers."
"Sammy?"
"A few books."
Snoopy tapped her chin in thought.

"You seem to always think about who gave what to you, and you always list them like that. I think that you're afraid of losing more people in your life and adding the wrong people to it. Like how Archie and that girl hit it off on their first date. You're worrying if you made the right choice or not to help him."

I looked at her. "How did you know that it was his first date? And that I helped him?"

"Some people are so predictable. What's the girl's name?"

"Jordan."

"Nice. Now skedaddle."

"Thanks, Snoopy."

"Yo' welcome."

I was thinking about her amazing way of seeing through people when I realized I was still chatting with my friends. It turns out that they were starting a little game of *Lore Legends,* and I didn't join yet.

I joined the game and slipped on my headphones.

"Where were you? We were dying out there!" I could hear Tharisa yelling in my ear. "My avatar needs serious escape tips!"

Chapter 21
World Peace

The next two months went by uneventful and short, so summer vacation came on pretty quick.

Today is the start of the last week of school, which was going to be celebrated with flags in a parade.

Luckily, we didn't have to wear traditional dress, which made the kid who got Russia breathe a sigh of relief.

I got Italy.

So basically, we spent half an hour each day marching around the cafeteria waving flags in the air.

Gorey Thompson, who got Brunei, pushed me to the end of the line because, and I quote, "You're farther than me har har har."

This caused some hazard issues.

On the day of the "parade," Borneo accidentally pushed Belgium with his flag, who pushed USA, who pushed Brazil, who pushed India, who then pushed Japan, who then pushed Switzerland, who then pushed Kenya—and it went on like that like a human domino chain.

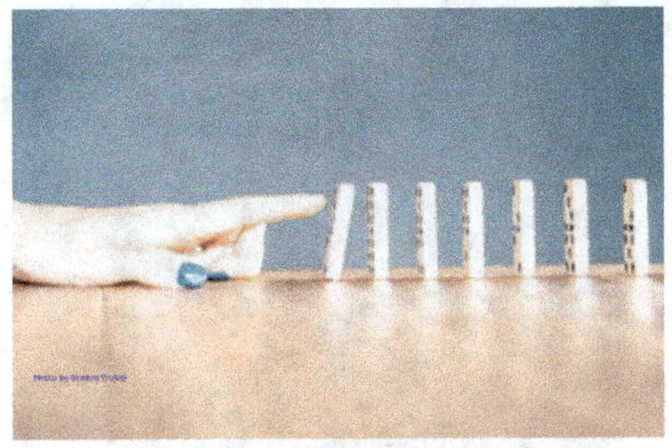

Luckily Italy was at the end of the single-file line.

Things got pretty heated from there because everyone accused each other of doing this on purpose and started hitting each other with the flag poles.

The teachers broke up the fight and, in the end, I got to keep all the flags.

Chapter 22
Farmer's Market

Summer's here.

On the first week of summer there is a little farmer's market/carnival in Jackson Park with a few stands where they sell you stuff and a Ferris wheel, which is the only ride that does not restrict you for being overage.

Jonah asked me to help him set up his grocery stand at the fair and stand in for him when he is not available.

I agreed when he offered me part of the payment.

We had to drag everything to the park because no Uber would let us bring four baskets and three coolers of food into his car.

"I'm giving a bad review on Yelp!" Jonah threatened as the fourth Uber drove away.

We miraculously managed to bring every piece of brand food to the fair without a car by 11:00 am, including the stand itself.

Jonah set up his sign that he designed at home while I set up a pitcher of lemonade:

JONAH'S GROCERY
All the good stuff in one stand!
Every item is $5!
Try the Senorita bread!
Lemonade is $1 a cup!

"That's a nice sign. I would like to put it up on my wall." I commented.

"You can! I made copies at home!" said Jonah.

"Really?"

"Sure! Consider it a bonus."

"Wow. Thanks."

"Hey look! It's Archie and Jordan."

"They're not canoodling, are they?"

"No, thank god, they're just buying strawberries. You can look."

"Hey! They are canoodling!"

"They weren't earlier! Turn around!"

"I feel sorry for Mr. Miller's Strawberries' customers."

"Okay. They're done now."

"Really?"

"Yeah. It was just a peck."

"Hey, who are they looking at?"

"They're looking at us."

"What are they saying?"

"Archie sayin' 'Hey Nellie's with a boy'. Then Jordan is sayin' 'How sweet!' Archie says, 'I don't think so.'"

"Bleh. The thought of me and you is just not possible. No offense."

"None taken."

"How do you know what they're saying? I can barely hear them."

"I learned lip reading."

"Huh."

"Archie is coming toward us."

"Okay. I'm fine with that."

"Hey Nellie. Hey Jonah." Archie and Jordan said in unison, except Archie said "Jonah" in a dark tone.

"Hello, *Lolo* and *Lola,*" Jonah replied, taking turns to take their right hands, and putting on his forehead. "*Mano po*, if you please."

Jordan gave him a little smile, and whispered to Archie "What the heck is he saying?"

Archie mouthed "I have not a hella idea."
He turned to me. "Whatcha doin' with this guy?" the dark tone returned.

"Selling brand food," I replied.

Archie nodded, turned Jordan's wheelchair in the opposite direction, and did that thing where he makes a peace sign and points it at his eyes and then points it back at me.

"What were you saying?" I asked, turning to Jonah.

"Go on Google Translate."

We sold all the brand food by 1:00 pm and used the money for some rounds on the Ferris wheel.

Chapter 23
Tahu

I went over to Tharisa's the next day.
I knocked on her door, she answered it.
"Just a sec," she said, and closed the door.
I could hear her grunting inside the house.
She opened the door again, panting. "A little help?" she asked.
I walked in, took my shoes off, and saw that Tharisa was trying to push Jordan up the stairs in her wheelchair.

Jordan looked a little embarrassed.
I ended up pushing along with Tharisa.
It took us thirty minutes to push Jordan up the stairs.

"Thank you, *Hiu*. Thanks, Nellie," Jordan said as she rolled down the hall.

"What's a hue?" I asked as Tharisa led me to her room.

"*Hiu*. It means 'shark'."

"Why did she call you that?"

"I look tough, but I don't want to hurt anyone."

"That's deep."

"I know, right?"

When I entered Tharisa's room, I saw a terrarium with a green snake inside.

"Aww. He's so cute," I said.

Obviously expecting me to be surprised, Tharisa concealed her excitement.

She picked him up. "This is Tahu," she said.

Before I could ask, Tharisa said, "That means 'know.'"

"Why did you name him that?"

"Because…well, if I tell you, you won't believe me."

"Hit me."

"Well, when I got him, I put him near my bed, and I could hear him talking to me, like telepathy. At first, I thought I was dreaming, but I opened my eyes, and he was transmitting words into my head! Jordan doesn't hear him, so she doesn't believe me."

"What does he say?"

"Where to get girl scout cookies."

"Useful."

"And what to print in the school newspaper."

"I believe you."

"You do?"

"Yeah. Sounds like your snake is possessed by a clairvoyant."

"Cool. Wanna see past issues of the school newspaper?"

"Sure. Maybe we can re-publish them in the fall."

"Perfect."

The Weekly Post

ESCAPE ROOM OPEN ON CALLOS STREET

Only $4 per person, and has four levels of escape rooms, Escapade Palace has brain stuff for all!
With varieties of head-

scratchers with live animals, lasers, and paintball booby traps. Even Rubik's cubes
and Super Mario. Mancala and technology.

The Weekly Post

INDOOR POOL GETS HEATING PADS AT JERONSKI'S COUNTRY CLUB

Hallelujah! Now when you step in Jeronski's blue pool you don't have to move to get warm!

CRAB MADE OF PLASTIC IN KOCHI, INDIA

Go green! (We didn't get the rights to remove the watermarks.)

<u>The Weekly Post</u>

BRAND FOOD PACKAGING LEADS TO TRIGGERS IN THE MIND TO BUY IT

Love the display on the Oreo-O's? You must like diabetes! Do the brands in the photo on the left catch your eye? Then you are destined for puffiness and kidney problems!!

DOGS UP FOR ADOPTION

Send away for one or two of these puppers!

Address

____

Name

____

The Weekly Post

LET'S GET REAL: EVERYTHING IS FOR RENT, EVEN A PUPPY!

Chapter 24
Happy Birthday, Archie

June 15th is Archie's Birthday.

Today was June 14th, and I still don't have a present.

"Maybe a goldfish?" suggested Jonah on the phone.

"Too fragile," I said.

"Chocolate?"

"That could work, but Tharisa said that Jordan was going to give that."

"Wine?"

"Where would I find wine on short notice?"

"Walgreens?"

"Give me a break, Jonah. And why wine?"

"Lots of grown-ups give wine as gifts. My dad has eight siblings, and each of them gave him a case of wine for Christmas! We still have seven boxes at the bottom of the pantry."

"Can I buy some from you?"

"Of course! Now, what I would suggest is the Brunello de Montepulciano. It has a taste that you want to swirl around your tongue for a few minutes, and is a very soft and smooth wine—"

"How do you know that?"

"My dad made me memorize this speech so he can record me in my wedding suit in a desperate attempt to sell the wine on eBay," he said in a gloomy tone.

"Yeah, tell him to hire Archie. And I'll take the Brunello de Montepulciano."

"How did you possibly pronounce that?"

"Because I'm in a desperate attempt to look good at his party tomorrow."

"Okay. Let me get it."

There was a rustling sound coming from my phone.

"Okay, bad news…" Jonah's voice sounded squeaky. "It turns out that someone else bought all seven cases of wine, and my dad already shipped it off."

"What type of person would buy seven cases of wine at once?"

"Alcoholics?"

"Never mind. Jonah, is there anything else that you can sell me that is not brand food?"

"Well…there is, but your options aren't pretty."

He texted me some photos.

I looked at them and sighed.

"Okay, I'll take a box."

###

June 15th.

Guests for Archie's party started to arrive at 11:00 am, but my order from Jonah hasn't.

Tanellio, Jordan, Cassandra, Hank, David, Baxter, and Amber were the only friends Archie had, and the only guests at his party besides me and Daneisha.

Hank and David arrived last and were carrying seven cases of wine as they walked through the door.

"Whoa!" Archie helped balance the load. "Where did you get these?"

"Some weirdos on eBay." David said, setting the case down on the table. "Seven cases of wine for twenty bucks! I kinda felt sorry for the poor sap's son.

He had to talk about the wine in a sad little suit. What's wrong with your sister?"

Archie turned to see me banging my head on the table while muttering "Brunello de Montepulciano".

I stopped when Archie glared at me.

Cassandra was helping Jordan position her wheelchair to align with the couch.

Jordan gave her present to Archie. "I got you chocolates."

Archie gave her a peck.

Daneisha covered my face with one of her hands.

Jordan added a side note. "Can we let my sister inside now?"

I opened the door where Tharisa was standing directly in front of, and she looked mad, with her fists clenched.

"*Anda beruntung bahwa pacar saudara perempuan saya atau saya akan memukuli Anda dengan sangat buruk*!" she yelled at Archie as she walked in.

Daneisha mouthed "what is she saying?"

"You're lucky that you're my sister's boyfriend or I would beat you up so bad," I translated.

"You know Indonesian?" Daneisha asked.

"No, but that's one of the possibilities of what she is saying right now."

Baxter handed his gift to Archie.

Fake mustaches.

"What is this, a white elephant?" David shouted.

"I have a gift for you!" said Hank and gave him a hug. Everybody laughed.

David handed his gift over.

"David, you hella cruel!" Archie nudged him playfully.

"Hey, your favorite movie is *Up*, so now you can look like Russel!" David commented.

I really don't get what college students say these days.

Amber waved an envelope in the air.

"I got you a Rock-Climbing World membership, but only for two months."
Archie high-fived her.

"Hey! My gifts' here!" Cassandra threw something at Archie.

Archie caught them.

Tanellio lifted a crate.

"I got you some groceries from that weird kid next door."

Archie took the crate and set it down.

Daneisha imitated Cassandra by throwing her present, a book, at Archie. He caught it again with one hand.

Tharisa sighed and rolled her eyes. "I have to give you a present, too." she said to Archie.

She reached into her backpack and pulled out a Funko Pop.

She threw it at Archie forcefully.

Archie was good at catching things.

Then the doorbell rang. I went to get it.

"Jonah! Where have you been?" I asked. He was standing in the doorway, holding a wide pan with what appeared to be thick rice noodles with orange sauce topped with some sliced eggs, chives, shrimp, and grounded pork rinds. Sammy was standing beside him.

"I made the mistake of telling my mom about Archie's birthday. She made me help her make this Filipino dish *Palabok*. But she burned the noodles, so she had to drive to Jollibee and get him a fast-food version instead.

Then my elderly *Lola* Garcia needed help figuring out my computer,
and then all my *Kuyas* and *Ates* trashed my room, so I had to clean up—"

"How many people live in your house, Jonah Osgood?" Sammy asked.

Archie heard the commotion and joined us at the door.

He didn't look too happy to see Jonah.

Jonah looked up at him. "Happy Birthday *Lolo*. My *Nanay* made…erm, bought you *Palabok* from Jollibee."

Archie made a confused look on his face.

"It's the best Filipino fast-food chain in the world! You'll like it!" Jonah explained, his eyes sparkling.

I bet that he would have performed a little dance recital or made rainbows with his hands if he wasn't holding a giant pan.

Reluctantly, Archie took the pan.

"I got you a Poké Ball." Sammy handed over her gift.

Archie took the Poké Ball and went back to his party.

Sammy handed me a box. "I helped Jonah carry this stuff on my way here."

I went to the party.

"Happy Birthday, Archie!" I said, plastering on a cheesy grin.

I don't usually use a cheery voice, so I could tell everybody was a little creeped out.

Archie took the box from me and opened it. "Thanks!".

I was glad he didn't think my gift was crappy:

Suddenly, I heard a screech, but I couldn't see anyone's mouth moving. Or anyone's face moving.

I realized the scream was coming inside my head. I put my hands over my ears, somehow thinking that would help. I grabbed a soda from off the table and started chugging.

I turned on my heel to the pantry, feeling around the brands to see if there was another guinea pig, but no luck.

I marched up to my room. I couldn't trust my senses. So, I have to do something to break them out of this frenzy.

I came back five minutes later, the scream guiding me, with my Ouija board under my arm.

Chapter 25
I'll Make It Up to You

I set the board down on the table. Nobody was impressed at this act, but Sammy turned pale.

"What are you going to do? Summon Mr. Puft?" David was making jokes.

"Tell me the name of a dead person." I said.

"Mr. Puft." David kept on going.

I was going to say *Shut up* but decided against it.

"Never mind. ""Joe Garseph was a toymaker. He made brilliant inventions for young and old. But his brother, jealous John, set his house on fire while Joe was still inside. Joe was dead."

Everyone grew quiet.

"But jealous John got pulled into the fire by his brother, so his inventions remain, but his voice doesn't. A new house was built on top of the burned one. This one." My voice grew darker.

"Archie, is your sister okay?" Amber mouthed.

The wind picked up outside and entered the house along with a few leaves. The iris from my eyes disappeared, leaving only the whites.

The wind rippled my hair as I spoke.

"Έλα παλιό φίλο. Έλα παλιό φίλο."

So, I guess Amber was half-right.

"Συμμετοχή. Γράφω."

Even though my irises were gone, I see that every college, high, and middle school student was looking at me like I was having a seizure; terrified.

Cassandra tried to make things normal again. "So do we just put our hand on the compass thing or—?"

She didn't need to.

The glass moved by itself.

"Hello."

"It's a pleasure that you turned 23, Archie."

"I'm so sorry about your parents."

By now, everyone looked petrified.

"I love your taste in furniture."

"Hopefully it doesn't burn to the ground like mine."

"Respect the little girl with the white eyes for knowing my story."

"I enjoyed making toys."

"If only I could live again."

"You sweet little kids deserve some caramel apples."

"I suppose you didn't see the basement yet?"
"Oh yeah. That fiasco with that parrot? Ugh. he was micturating everywhere."
"Anyway, got to go."
"Remember, the basement."

My irises returned to my eyes, but by that time, I felt like passing out.

Archie, Cassandra, Hank, David, Amber, Jordan, Baxter, Tanellio, Daneisha, Jonah, Tharisa, and Sammy were pure white.

Sammy snapped out of it before anyone else.

"Umm…been there done that got the t-shirt?" she said awkwardly.

I passed out.

Chapter 26
Animals

I woke up the next day, wondering what I did the day before.

Oh yeah, I thought. *I passed out during spirit summoning. Geez, that stuff just kicks into you.*

On second thought, realized that I just imagined all the laughing and that my synesthesia was acting up again.

But I got confused when everything on my shelf, except my Ouija board, Chromebook and all my books, disappeared.

I stared at my shelf, the only things that have disappeared were the toys from Snoopy and the Kiwi Crates and Little Passport kits.

I picked up a book that Sammy got for me.

Oh yeah. The guy. I thought.

I went downstairs. I was surprised that Archie didn't burn my Ouija board.

Archie was downstairs, sipping coffee, talking to Daneisha.

"I don't know how, but the plush pretzel and those fake mustaches that I got last night? They disappeared."

"It's probably that ghost that Nellie summoned." Daneisha said.

I walked to the kitchen and took out some cereal.

I checked for a guinea pig as a joke, but a light brown, orange guinea pig scampered out the Frosted Flakes as I poured into the mug.

I named him "Soccer" for no particular reason.

I put him in the basket with Oreo and they played tug-of-war with a piece of sunny-side-up and some toast.

Archie took off his glasses and rubbed his forehead when I told him about Soccer.

"Great. Another mouth to feed," he said.

"You know, all my toys disappeared last night." I said.

"Mine too, except the Poké Ball."

"I heard. Also, we're out of Cup of Cake."

"What? I just bought some yesterday!"

"Weird. The cupboard's empty."

I wasn't going to eat out of a cereal box a guinea pig probably lived in, so took out a box of miniature cookies to replace as cereal.

But as I poured, a blue and gold macaw flew out of the box and toppled over the milk.

I decided I was done with breakfast.

I named the parrot "Cookie" for obvious reasons and tied some wire racks together to make a cage.

This was weird.

A Hyacinth macaw burst out of my Greek yogurt later that afternoon.

Well, "Hyacinth" had to share the cage with Cookie.

I had a weird feeling that this was about climate change.

Chapter 27
Joe Garseph's Reward

I consulted with Jane to clean my foodie animals because they reeked, and they had to stay in my room, according to Archie.

Jane charged five dollars.

I walked back home to solve the mystery about the disappearance of my toys.
Archie definitely didn't burn them because my Ouija board was still there.

I started wondering about the word "toy." It wandered in my mind like a lost kid in a grocery store.

This reminded me of the toymaker Joe Garseph, then I remembered that I summoned him yesterday.

I remembered that he said something about the basement.

I decided to check it out.

I opened the door to the basement and walked down the steps.

They creaked with each heavy foot placed.

The basement was empty, with no boxes of spare stuff, but I felt the urge to keep walking.

It was like I stepped onto an invisible force field line, because when I stepped on it, a green, white, yellow, orange, red and blue mess of toys surrounded the room. It included Archie's and my toys that disappeared.

I noticed an engraving on the wooden floor.

TO THE WHITE-EYE

I marched up the steps and told Archie that I found his birthday gifts.

Archie followed me down the basement and was happy to be reunited with a stuffed pretzel.

"I think that Joe Garseph got us some gifts for summoning him." I pointed at the engraving.

"These toys were invented by Joe Garseph." Archie looked at the pile.

I held out Archie's plush, but when he touched it, he ricocheted into the wall.

Luckily, Archie is pretty sturdy, so all he did was lie down and groan.

"Are you dead?" I asked.

"Ughh. No, I'm fine," Archie responded weakly.

"I think it's a curse. Joe the toymaker here must have wanted to only give this to me."

"Keep the pretzel. I don't want to die." Archie groaned again.

Archie was able to stagger up, walk to the living room, and lie down again on the couch.
I carried the stuff to my room while Archie coached me about where to put which.

I found out on the internet that Archie was right; all the items were made by Joe Garseph.

I still had a chocolate pig in the freezer, so I sacrificed it in thanks.

Contract making with spirits is mandatory, and very different from the ones that Archie signs to pay the electricity bill.

Chapter 28
Chocolate and Pure Luck

Tharisa came over to my house to find out that Daneisha was terrified of snakes, as she brought Tahu with her.

"GET THAT THING AWAY FROM ME!" Daneisha overreacted, standing on the table with a broom in her hands.

Tharisa muttered "Wuss," and put Tahu in my room. Luckily, the snake was on the smallish side, so it was no harm to Oreo, Soccer, Hyacinth, and Cookie.

Still, I hid all four of them in my closet for safety measures.

I handed Tharisa a squeeze yogurt, checking for parrots first.

"Tahu told me about a new chocolate shop," Tharisa whispered in my ear. "He told me to come to your place. It existed in the 1960s, closed, and now it is opening again near Cacao."

"Then Lenny's going to have some competition." I replied. "What's the name of this chocolate shop?"

"I don't know. But for some reason, Tahu told me to look under Archie's bed."

"Is he a stalker?"

"How should I know?"

"I think we should look," I found myself saying.

"What?"

"I have a feeling…of having to do that."

"I've never been in a boy's room before."

"Me neither, but we should still do it."

Surprised by my sudden interest, Tharisa agreed.

"So, what's the plan?" she asked.

"I could cut my hand and call Archie. While he's taking care of me, you can sneak up to his room and look under the bed."

"NO! Nothing like that." Tharisa looked left and right. "Jordan is coming over in ten minutes, so it will be motivation for us to get away, and an excuse for Archie to come out of his room."

"That is a better plan."

After ten minutes, everything happened as Tharisa predicted.

We snuck up to Archie's room. I kept guard while Tharisa crawled under the bed.

But it turns out that I was thinner than Tharisa because I don't really work out that much, so we went vice versa.

Along with the Tommy Hilfiger, I saw under the bed a crack with a card stuck in it.

I pulled it out and crawled out of the bed.

Once outside, we biked to the location Tharisa described and parked in front of a sign.

I pulled out the piece of paper. I didn't bother to look at it earlier since we were in an unnecessary hurry.

It was blank.

I put it back in my pocket and followed Tharisa into the store.

The aroma of chocolate was hard to miss.

I looked at the card again. I saw a colorful display of the store's contents on the card.

I turned it over. Ten yellow circles on top of a blue background were printed on the back.

A middle-aged worker with a nose ring spotted it. "Where did you find that?"

I looked at Tharisa. She looked back. "On the street," she lied.

"That's the first punch card the company designed." The man stared in awe. "I can't believe it! I searched for a clean copy of this card even before I inherited this store!" he put his hands in the air.

"How much do you want for it?" he asked enthusiastically.

Tharisa, being the businessperson that she was, wrote a contract on a pad of paper and gave it to the man.

She smiled widely and effectively.

Soon, the card was in a small frame on the wall of the shop, and Tharisa and I were carrying a bag of chocolate, caramel apples, etc.

The bag was heavy but rewarding.

Chapter 29
Uncle Tad's Visit

Uncle Tad reads his emails, but he doesn't answer them.

I know this personally because instead of sending my birthday money through my account, he sends it in an envelope along with a few packs of gum.

Uncle Tad knocked on the door and waited outside.

Daneisha looked through the peephole and started putting furniture up against the door.

Uncle Tad came through the window instead.

Archie came down the steps and was shocked to see Uncle Tad.

"Hey, buddy! You said you needed help!" Uncle Tad yelled.

"Yeah, but that was in February. I'm good now. I actually sent you an email just now." Archie replied. "Would like some provisions? You can stay for a week if you want—"

"Actually, uh, your Aunt Luisa, uh, kicked me out." Uncle Tad's voice was scratchy, but that was just inherited. "Can I live here?"

Uncle Tad slipped on a puppet sock that he glued red yarn to. "Sure, Taddy! I'll be happy to keep you!" he mimed the sock before Archie could answer. "And we can be roommates!" he added.

Archie paused and marched up to his room, followed by Daneisha.

From the comfort of my room, I could hear Archie throwing his swivel chair and Daneisha screaming into a pillow.

I could hear them walking down the stairs again and that they were saying that Uncle Tad had to stay in my room.

That night wasn't a happy picnic.

Uncle Tad's snores could rival the noise of an air-raid siren.

It was 1:00 am and I still couldn't sleep.

The wind picked up in my room until it blew in a circle around the four walls.

Uncle Tad woke up to see me staring at him with eyes without irises.

He ran out screaming louder than his snores, picking up his bag and practically flying out the door.

His screams were still heard when he ran out into the streets.

It woke up Archie and Daneisha, too, but by then I was already asleep.

To:tad_gravel@gmali.com
From:archie_consaita@gmali.com

Dear Uncle Tad,

Good news! I have a great group of friends!
Good news! You don't have to come here anymore!
We got it all taken care of!

Sincerely,
Archie

Chapter 30
The Snake

Daneisha has an impressive collection of Funko Pops but has really bad taste in organization.

Archie was teaching her about color coordination in her room while I munched on some fudge downstairs.

Sammy called me and asked if I wanted to walk to the creek.

I agreed, but only because there was a presence of a person I did not know, lurking around the house.

Sammy added on the phone call that we were going to do "professional wading."

I grabbed my bucket and told Archie that I was going down to the creek, to which he replied ""Kay, enjoy your youth."

I met Sammy at the creek to see her in a suit made of bubble wrap.

She answered before I could ask. "We're doing professional wading. We need proper attire. Oh, and BTW I brought Jonah."

Jonah waved. "Who wants to play 'who can kill the most *langaw* and put it in a plastic bag'?" he asked. "I'm in the lead. I caught about ten already." He held up a plastic bag with a couple of dead flies inside.

Sammy, looking revolted but trying not to be rude by Jonah's way of life, said, "No thanks.", and focused on me.

She reached into a duffle bag and pulled out a red suit.

I tried it on and looked ridiculous.

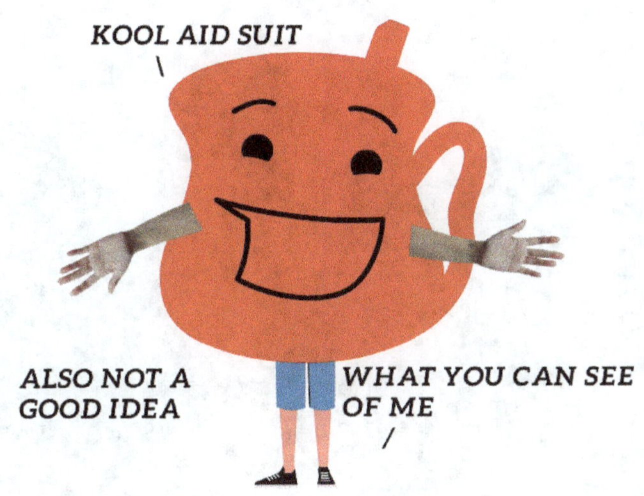

Sammy made a short laugh. "I didn't have any other bubble wrap suits, but I did have my last Halloween costume."

I took it off, which was pretty hard, considering that I looked like Kool-Aid Man. "I'll just get my pants wet." I said, even though I was wearing shorts.

I waded in the creek after Sammy, whose bubble wrap suit actually did keep her clothes dry.

"Ooh, I caught a frog." Sammy held up her bucket.

Jonah, still on land, put on a mask and waded into the water. He explained that it was to scare off trespassers so we could have the lake to ourselves. He had four different types of masks in the duffle bag.

I told him that I had the same ones at home and suggested that maybe he should try the spitting llama hat instead that I picked it up from Snoopy yesterday.

Sammy caught another frog.

"Hey, less chatting, more catching." Sammy barked at us.

Jonah caught an axolotl in his bucket.

A very weird discovery, considering that Mexico was a handful of a thousand miles from where we were standing.

I, sadly, caught another snake.

I decided to just let it go and try to catch an actual frog like normal people, but then I realized it had another head.

Sammy caught a glimpse of the snake and threw her bucket in the air.

It landed in the water, helping the frogs escape back to their creek.

Sammy struggled to catch the frogs again while I set my specimen, still in the bucket, down on the grass.

Sammy couldn't return the frogs to her bucket, so I gave her some Human Bacon Bits that I packed as comfort food (provided by Snoopy).

I fed a little to the snake, one piece for each head.

"Cerberus," I whispered.

Sammy polished off her bacon. We lay down in the shade of a big tree.

I reached into my pockets and pulled out some treats for Cerberus.

I took a picture of Cerberus, googled him, checked to see if he was venomous, he wasn't, then poured him back into the creek.

I snacked on some treats and dipped my feet into the creek.

That feeling of serenity felt so familiar.

There was a heartbeat of love in a known, yet unknown presence.

"Nellie?"

I turned around. Sammy and Jonah were staring at me. "You, okay?"

"Yeah."

"Hey, the killing flies' game is actually pretty fun." Sammy handed me a flyswatter.

We played for a half hour or so, then it was time to go home.

Except when I got home, there was no one around.

Chapter 31
Presence

With not a soul in sight, I looked around.

At first, I thought this was a prank, but the eerie silence told me it wasn't.

My first thought was *Well, I guess, I inherit everything now*, but I heard a sound coming from the basement. *Too Bad.*

I opened the door, only to be hit in the head with a book. I wasn't fazed, but it still was unexpected.

"Oh! Sorry!" I could hear Cassandra's voice from behind my hair.

I could see Daneisha, Amber, Tanellio, Baxter, Cassandra, Archie, Jordan, Hank, and David huddled together in one corner.

"Sorry. I thought that you were—" Cassandra paused, the color draining from her face.

I stared at everyone. Hank pointed a shaky finger, eyes wide as golf balls.

I felt a dim hand clamp on my shoulder.

The same feeling of serenity and the warm heartbeat of love returned to me.

I turned around to see a transparent body, so I could see the bones through her skin, but just barely.

Pale, moving swiftly in a tattered dress, she looked at me, smiled, and disappeared in a process of evaporation.

The next day, peculiarly, none of Archie's friends, nor Archie himself, including Daneisha, mentioned the ghastly figure or explained how it got into our house.

Chapter 32
Business Meeting

That day nobody mentioned the spirit was the day Archie came downstairs in a plaid shirt, camera around his neck and in contact lenses instead of glasses, so now he really does look like Archie Andrews.

Daneisha noticed his new look first. "What?" was all she said.

"Business meeting," Archie replied.

"Can you be more descriptive?"

Archie rolled his eyes, but that made his contacts fall out.

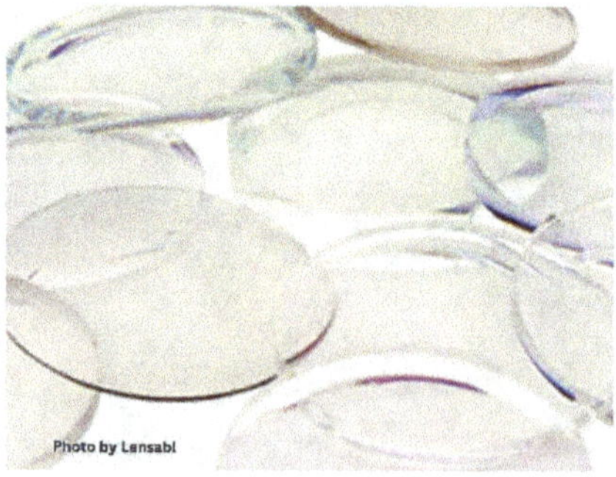

Archie, struggling to see, fumbled on the floor, feeling around for the two small disks. "The gang and I have a meeting with a company so they can buy us."

"You have a business?"

"Yeah. I finally finished my photo file. Haven't I told you about this yesterday? Oh, there it is."

Archie slipped on the contacts.

"Well, no one is going to take you seriously; you look like Archie had a fall out with Veronica.", I found myself saying.

I knew that Archie wanted to give me "the look," but he didn't want to lose his contacts again.

"Our business is called 'Color. Co'," he said. "And you're coming along."

Before I could ask, he said "People who are in their thirties tend to be more vulnerable around small children."

I wanted to remind him that I was twelve, but his contacts fell out again.

"Darn it!"

"Stick with the glasses and graphic tees," Daneisha suggested.

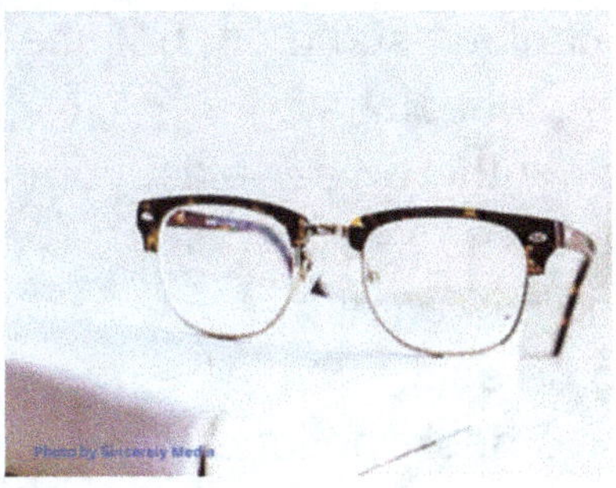

Archie staggered up the steps, holding onto the rail, went into his room, and came out looking like himself again.

"Who are you trying to get to buy you?" I asked on our way out.

"Photo.Co" he said, waving to an Uber.

"Very imaginative."

The Uber drove us to a nearby city, where it stopped in front of a large building.

Archie tipped the driver and walked into the lobby, where his little clique was waiting.

Tanellio waved both his hands up.

David pointed at me. "Why—?"

Cassandra nudged him before he could finish his question.

"Ow!"

"Let's be professional." she said.

Amber reached out and gave Hank a noogie.

Archie and Tanellio high-fived each other.

Jordan couldn't stand up, but she was able to low-five from her wheelchair.

"For twenty-three-year-olds, you all are acting like seventh graders." I said.

Everyone looked at me.

It had to be said.

A lady at a desk motioned for Archie's clique to ride up the elevator.

It was a struggle for eight college students, one in a wheelchair, and one middle schooler to fit inside a single elevator.

Baxter looked like he couldn't breathe, but luckily, our stop was only on the third floor.

I had to sit in a chair in a separate room while Color. Co was talking with a middle-aged woman in another room.

The doors were glass, so I could see what was happening, but then a security guard pulled down a shade in front of the doors, so I could only hear the conversation.

The security guard stood in front of the doors like an English guard, except his hat was shorter.

He stared at me like I was going to cause trouble.

I looked back at him, but only with my eyes half-shut.

I could hear the woman yelling at Color. Co through the very thin doors.

"YOU PHOTOGRAPH LIKE A (bad word) SIX-YEAR-OLD! WHAT'S WITH ALL THESE (bad word) COLORS! WHAT'S WITH THE (bad word) OBJECTS THAT YOU PHOTOGRAPH. (bad word). OUT OF ALL THE (bad word) MEAGER ITEMS OUT THERE YOU PHOTOGRAPH THIS!" I could tell she was holding up the photos of Joe Garseph's inventions and Jonah's many food brands. What a drama queen.

The wind picked up inside again, my hair got tossed in the process.

Again? I thought. *What for now?*

The woman was still yelling at Color. Co.

From what I could think of, Tanellio, Jordan, Cassandra, Baxter, Hank, David, Amber, and Archie were confused on why this weird lady was yelling at them, were cringing, and wanted to film a video of this woman.

"...AND YOU CAN THROW YOUR RESUMES OFF A VERY HIGH BUILDING! YOUR (bad word) IMMATURE COLOR COORDINATION SKILLS MUST HAVE BEEN INHERITED! YOU'RE NOT MAKING YOUR (bad word) MOTHER PROUD!"

At the word "mother," I could tell that Cassandra, Tanellio, Jordan, Baxter, Hank, Amber, and David were holding Archie back from punching the woman into a coma. I honestly thought that this loud woman was pathetic, but I guess some other people's feelings are more fragile.

The security guard fell asleep in the process of staring at me. The wind that picked up grew stronger.

The irises from my eyes disappeared again.

I marched up to the door, flung it open. The wind followed me.

The wind picked up the photographs the lady had crumpled with her fingernails, making a stable tornado of Color. Co's colorful advertisements.

With my white eyes and the wind whipping up my hair along with the pieces of paper, I looked, from the woman's point of view, very menacing.

The woman threw herself behind the desk, but the wind threw the desk over her shoulder.

She looked like a helpless guinea pig

She caught a piece of paper before it could get picked up by the tornado, signed it, and gave it to Archie.

"HERE! TAKE IT! YOU'RE BOUGHT! YOU'LL GET PAID! YOU HAVE GREAT COLOR TASTE! NOW GET HER OUTTA HERE!" she yelled and pointed at me.

The tornado settled down, my irises returned, and I fell asleep in the process.

Do you think anyone would laugh or cry in this situation?

Chapter 33
The Kid

The next day, Color. Co was putting together a gallery of photos for an in-person and online viewing.

While they were doing that in our living room, Jonah rang the doorbell and was rejected by Archie, who slammed the door in his face, almost breaking Jonah's nose bridge.

I re-answered the door. "You, okay?" I asked.

"Yea. I guessh sho." Jonah held his nose. I could see blood through the cracks of his fingers.

I gave him a tissue. He rolled it up and stuck it in his bleeding nostril. "I'm going wading again."

"I'll get my bucket."

###

The peace returned at the creek. Jonah took the tissue out of his nose and threw it in a nearby garbage can, but not before rinsing it in the creek.

It was not hard to recognize Cerberus in the crowd of snakes sunning themselves on the rocks.

Jonah mentioned that he caught a few things inside his bucket.

Photo credits via Unplash.com

"You're pretty good at catching these things." I commented.

Sammy parked her bike next to the tree and ran over with her bubble wrap suit.

"If you catch a frog, lemme know." she said.

"Why?" Jonah asked.

"So, I have a present that my cousin actually wants."

"You can give him some beer socks," Jonah added, "You must really hate your cousin."

"I do. And he comes every weekend."

"If it makes you feel better, I have eight sib-lings, nine cousins, one *Tita*, one *Tito*, one *Lola*, one *Lolo*, and one *Nanay* and *Tatay*. We all live under the same roof."

"Tough love."

"Yeah."

Sammy caught a crayfish and put it in her bucket.

"I'll trade you a frog for the crayfish." Jonah pointed at his bucket. Inside was a fat bullfrog.

"Deal," Sammy said. They traded buckets. "What're gonna do with him?"
"Eat him."

Sammy took back her bucket.
"What are you? 'The Kid.'", she asked.
"Who is the kid?"
I broke in. "'The Kid' comes here at night, naked, catches crayfish with his bare hands, ten every handful, and eats them alive. He picks berries from that bush over there and eats the ones with insects on it. He once brought his brother and sister here and pushed them in the creek."
Sammy and Jonah stared at me. "How do you know that?" Jonah asked.
"Dumb lies Archie told me when I was a kid." I said.
I showed them a photo on my phone.

"You drew this as a small child?" Jonah asked.
"...Yeah. Sure," I replied.
I'm very bad at drawing.

Chapter 34
Eliete

The next day it rained.

Archie was drinking tea at the bar, finally taking a break from his gallery page.

Photo by Massimo Rinaldi

"Why can't we order pizza?" Daneisha called from the couch.

"You sold all of our plates and bowls." Archie replied, taking another sip.

"The pizza place provides paper plates."

"We'll revisit the subject later."

In all of my pure luck, the great inventions that I have learned about, my white eyes, the snow, the pets, and my two siblings, I found myself asking a question I thought that I would never think about.

"What is mom's first name?"

Archie gagged on his tea. He set the cup down and rubbed his temples.

"Eliete," he said. "Ell-ee-ett-ttay," he repeated.

"Speaking of names," Daneisha called from the couch again. "We need to change our last names to 'Bly' again. They're still 'Consaita'."

"Damn, Nellie, you're ahead of us," Archie said. He went back to drinking his tea.

"Well…then the spirit that 'attacked' you the other day…" I began awkwardly. "…that was mom."

Archie spit out his tea. Daneisha fell off the couch, both acting like cartoon characters.

"I mean…think about it," I continued. "When you were failing that meeting, she possessed me temporarily and you got bought. And she helped Daneisha and I actually…bond with each other. And she helped me entertain your guests."

Archie and Daneisha stared at me. I was used to people staring at me by now.

Since nobody else was saying anything, I continued again. "And I saw a photo on your desk; she looked a lot like me, and the ghost looked the same thing…"

I trailed off. Daneisha, regaining control of her mouth, finished her path of thought.

"She's been with us the whole time."

I ran upstairs, grabbed my Ouija board, and set it on the table.

Minutes passed. The piece began to move.

"You finally figured it out, hon?"

Archie clapped his hands over his mouth.

"You all are such great kids. You deserve everything."

The same figure from Chapter 31 appeared through the walls, ever floating.

"Hi, Mom," Daneisha waved.

Archie leaned in for a hug, only to pass right through her.

"Face it, Archie. You're only here for comic relief." Daneisha laughed.

BLY FAMILY TREE

© Amelie Fajardo

COLOR. CO PHOTO GALLERY

PHOTO CREDITS: JORDAN ARYA

PHOTO CREDITS: ARCHIE BLY

PHOTO CREDITS: HANK BOHAM

PHOTO CREDITS: DAVID CEST

PHOTO CREDITS: CASSANDRA DARYL

PHOTO CREDITS: TANELLIO KURTULUSH
AND BAXTER HASE

PHOTO CREDITS: AMBER WAN

Epilogue
Everyone Gets Happy

So now that we are reunited with my mother, she makes us breakfast every day, which is a good thing.

Jonah partnered up with Grace Kennedy, a girl who was a grade up above him who likes to make hats and socks.

And *Jonah's Groceries and Grace's Hats* were a big success.

Color.Co won a scholarship for college so they could slave away less, so Archie could finally get his own car.

The year Archie turned twenty-four I gave him a better present.

It turns out the yelling woman from Photo.Co was named Ms. Thisby, and Archie was still pretty sore about the "mother proud" comment.

For his twenty fourth birthday I took him and all of Color.Co back to the Photo.Co building, along with Tharisa.

Color.Co watched Tharisa Arya through the glass doors slap Ms. Thisby in the face.

"Face Shot! Four hundred points," David shouted.

Ms. Thisby didn't notice Color.Co through the glass, so she didn't know where this strange little child came from and couldn't blame Color.Co.

Daneisha got into college to be a chocolatier, which I guess with all the chocolate shops there are in the neighborhood, was a little obvious.

I find myself fifteen years later still working for Tharisa as a journalist for a newspaper company that she started, *Neighborhood Watch*.

I was the only one that actually understood her tough image because of her pet name, *Hiu*.

Once in a while, Jonah, Sammy, Tharisa and I would get together and catch up on each other's lives, as Sammy was now a pediatrician and still hated teenagers and *Jonah's Market* was started two years earlier.

And Jonah now has a bigger selection of brand food to stock his stand.

And our first taste of wine was disgusting.

I don't know how Archie and other adults like that stuff and how some actually get addicted to it.

Coffee was pretty bad, too, so instead we continued drinking milk to this day, even though we all are less lactose-tolerant than before.

On a side note, I got to keep Cerberus, who actually was pretty sturdy because he is still alive. As for Cookie, Hyacinth, Oreo, and Soccer, I gave them to Jane Wazzer when I turned thirteen.

On another side note: earlier that year Archie got married to Jordan.

So, I guess that those two were made for each other.

If you have never been to a wedding before, I can tell you firsthand; it's long.

I wasn't part of the ceremony, so all I did was sit in a lawn chair for two hours until the buffet.

Tharisa sat in the back and caught two hours of sleep.

The only entertaining part of the wedding was when an escaped elephant somehow wandered into the buffet table.

So, I guess that means that there is just a nice little ending to everything.

But seriously. Don't drink coffee. It's gross.

At least, mom is there to make me breakfast every day.

NEIGHBOORHOOD WATCH:
LUCK ON THE SIDEWALKS—by Nellie Bly

Firts thing, my mom is immortal because she can't die again, and I guess that is inherted.

Also, our editor is lousy on etding tihs. Thakns a lot, Helena.

So, I guess it started when I was a little kid, young age of twelve, I start seing things.

I guess I didn't tel anyone, thinking tha they would think I'm crazy, or I thought it was synthesia, but I guess my mother was always there.

Archie, my older brother, was defintly teased as a kid for being named after a famous comic book character, but by the time he went to college he found good freinds and a girlfriend that apprecaietes his quirks and started a photography and advertisement and color consultant business called Color.Co.

Last summer, Archie got married to Jordan, so now Tharisa is my sister and my boss, so yeah, cool.

My older sister, Daniesha, used to hate me when I was a kid, but finding Archie a grilfiernd bonded us together.

I admit that Snoopy was right, I was a little afraid of losing more than I had itnented, but for now i'll enjoy the process.

When i fall flat on my face sometimes, thanks to Sammy, I don't bleed because the pavement is made of cake, Metaforicaly speaking.

Oreo, my old pet guinea pig, could eat human food im guessing due to the chemicals we spray on the grass.

Or maybe because we have a fake lawn made of plastic, I dont know.

Jonah, my friend of the opposite sex, is Filipino, as I found out years later, and i was able to get a tagalog-english dictionary at the bookstore.

He still plays the kill the fly game, but accoplished taking over Goodway and living the dream selling brand food.

By best friend, Sammy, was beaten by kids who were two years younger than us. But she is humble about it now.

On a side note, she still loathes teenagers, having experienced being one for a couple of years and hating it.

In summary, life happens.

—Bly

ACKNOWLEDGEMENTS

Thanks to:

My *Nanay* & *Tatay*

My childhood playroom

The stories that keep me up all night

Sally the succulent & Planty the fiddle-leaf fig plant

Ms. Carla & Jonah

Hunka Chunka Monkey by Sam E. Bromley
The Loch Ness Monster

Kimba, for my most cherished childhood adventures
with Conexiones Institute
Ms. Kim Brae, my kindergarten teacher

Hickman ECs & staff
(from 1st to 8th grade):
- Ms. Diane, my former homeschool EC,
  and Ms. Jennifer my current one,
- Ms. Danaan, Ms. Elizabeth, and Ms. Jane,
- Ms. Jaine, Ms. Lauren, and Ms. Leah,
- Ms. Marla, Ms. Megan, and Ms. Melissa

Writopia & Kumon, for my reading and writing classes

Branelius, your books compelled me to write this book

Reading Room & Le Carrousel at Bryant Park, NYC
Umpire Rock at Central Park, NYC

chocolates

You all helped create and inspire
the big and small details of this book.

ABOUT THE AUTHOR

Amelie Fajardo is a kid author by heart. She is a prolific writer with the grandest, richest, and most vibrant imagination. From a young age, she has been an avid reader and her love for writing is insatiable. As always, she takes great delight in telling stories with such passion and diligence, particularly one that she has just finished writing.

Amelie is ecstatic for her first published book, Bly, and it is her absolute dream come true!

Matilda by Roald Dahl is one of her favorite books amongst many others.

She is also a natural creative and finds joy in exploring various art forms. Almost always, her literary works are accompanied by her original illustrations.

The world is her playground! She loves to travel and gets her inspiration for writing from the places she visits. In this book, the town where Nellie Bly lives is influenced by bits and pieces of the quaint old town of Tehachapi, CA, and the laidback urban life of Washington DC.